Dread Empress Of All

The Oceans

INKLET #77

LIANA BROOKS

www.inkprintpress.com

Print ISBN: 978-1-922434-17-3
eBook ISBN: 9798201393847

www.inkprintpress.com

National Library of Australia Cataloguing-in-Publication Data
Brooks, Liana 1982 –
Dread Empress Of All The Oceans
48 p.
ISBN: 978-1-922434-17-3
Inkprint Press, Canberra, Australia
1. Fiction—Fantasy—Contemporary 2. Fiction—Sea Stories 3. Fiction—Short Stories

First Print Edition: March 2022
Cover photo © Membio via Deposit Photos
Cover design © Inkprint Press
Interior art © Amy Laurens

Dread Empress Of All The Oceans

LIANA BROOKS

OTHER WORKS

ALL I WANT FOR CHRISTMAS

All I Want For Christmas Is A Reaper
All I Want For Christmas Is A Werewolf

FLEET OF MALIK

Bodies In Motion
Change of Momentum

HEROES AND VILLAINS

Even Villains Fall In Love
Even Villains Go To The Movies
Even Villains Have Interns
Even Villains Play The Hero (books 1 – 3 omnibus)
The Polar Terror

TIME AND SHADOWS

The Day Before
Convergence Point
Decoherence

SHORTER WORKS

Fey Lights
Prime Sensations
Darkness and Good

Find other works by the author at
www.lianabrooks.com

DREAD EMPRESS OF ALL THE OCEANS

"Honey." My husband caught my eye and nodded behind me as the 6-year-old twins we were trying to corral squealed with delight.

I turned, pausing in my duties as Applier Of The Sunscreen to look for what had brought my husband on high alert. It was a beach between the Gulf of Mexico and Choctawhatchee Bay, anchored and shaded by the causeway overhead. The Emerald Coast Parkway ran the length of the Florida panhandle, from Fort Walton Beach to the bend of Apalachee Bay. It was the land of tourists, trinket shops, and our family's favorite destination for escaping the oppressive summer heat of Lower Alabama.

Vivid blue skies. White sand. Emerald green water turned dark by sea grass and sparkling with tiny silver fish.

The sign said Redneck Beach and I said it was the closest I'd get to saltwater while my children were young.

If anyone asked, I said I was terrified of riptides. But what really scared me was the two stunningly handsome men drawing curious glances under the failing shade of the bridge. It was only nine; in an hour the sun would be too high to give the parking lot on the south of the bridge any shade. I should have checked the time.

The tide must be coming in.

"Just go talk to them," my husband

said. "You know how they are."

"Why isn't spear-hunting legal?" I muttered.

"Mom!" The oldest was ten and absolutely horrified. Our family was mostly vegetarian, not exactly a difficult thing to do when we lived in the southern United States with nine months of growing season and lived on a vegetable farm with an orchard. We kept chickens and ate the occasional fish or deer in the winter when neighbors overstocked their freezers, but beyond that our hunting didn't go much past chasing blackberries in the brambles.

Grumbling under my breath I passed the twin I was pinning down to his big sister. "Finish putting sunscreen on him and don't forget his ears! Your father's people burn."

My husband chuckled. Easily burnt skin was probably his only failing in life.

I kissed his cheek and went to face the music.

The two men were tall, broad shouldered, deeply tanned with sun-bleached, wave-tousled hair and striking blue-green eyes that would have won them any number of lovers or movie contracts if that's what they desired. I'd known them both since I was fourteen and my grandfather—in what was retrospectively the worst decision an adult could make—took me to the beach after my mother's funeral.

As I approached, both men straightened, eyes widening in delight and hope.

Once upon a time I was pretty, even beautiful when I tried to be. My hair was thick and wavy, a rich chocolate-brown with sun-kissed gold highlights. I had long legs. I had dark eyes. I had a nice rack. And after having twins and knee problems I was also sixty some pounds over what was considered a fashionable weight and at least twenty pounds over a healthy weight.

Which is my way of saying that in my black-and-white one-piece suit I looked more like a beached orca than a Beach Babe.

You couldn't tell from looking at how these guys reacted.

The leader of the pack stepped forward, and it was a pack. That's the correct name for a group of sharks and while only two were on land, there would be more in the water.

"You have finally returned to us." He put a hand over his heart and I tried to remember what I'd called him. Ray, maybe?

"I haven't returned. I'm here to swim with my family."

"Of course," Ray said. "We'll clear the beach and the waters."

I had to grab his arm to keep him

from leaving and turning the tide red with the blood of mangled tourists. "No. No, not required. I'm just going to swim here. Like this. And you can go do your thing. How is the whole democracy working out for you?"

Both sets of blue-green eyes went black with anger.

Fish don't like democracies it turns out.

They like apex predators, leaders, monarchs.

They like blood curses that fall upon the eldest daughter to the eldest daughter until the moon ceases to shine.

They like things that make for good stories and poor life choices.

At fourteen, the now only surviving eldest daughter of the eldest daughter, they'd offered me a chance to rule a kingdom under the waves.

Castles. Servants. Flippers. Magic. Breathing underwater. A truly staggering amount of pink pearls...

And I had run screaming from the beach because none of that was going to let me make the volleyball team.

In time I'd convinced myself that it was a hallucination brought on by depression and heatstroke. Until I came for a moonlit walk on the beach with my college boyfriend and had to rescue him from drowning while we were on the pier. He was attacked by an ocean wave.

The news said it was a freak mini-tsunami.

I called it malicious attack by merfolk.

"We've discussed this," I said with a polite smile. "I'm not interested in ruling anything. Neither was my mother. Or her mother. Or her mother. You might have gotten that from the way the Chosen One keeps avoiding ruling you every generation."

Ray gnashed his teeth together.

Fish also have long memories. "Our world needs a ruler."

"Great! Go pick someone from your world to rule," I suggested. "I'm happy here."

They looked dubiously at my husband.

He was pushing 40, developing a slight middle-aged paunch, had a receding hairline, laughing brown eyes, and an easy smile. So perfect! Not conventionally handsome, maybe, but he'd been my best friend in school. Supported me through everything. Made me laugh when the world was bleak. And when I'd told him I was the destined queen of a watery kingdom he'd taken it in stride.

"You could do better," Ray said.

"I could also do far worse. He loves me. I love him. We have kids and an orchard. We're happy."

"But what of us, my queen?" Ray looked at me pleadingly.

Ocean water lapped over my feet, climbing far higher than the tideline suggested it should.

I kicked the wave away like it was an annoying dog. "What insurmountable problem has you swimming this close to the bay?"

The two men exchanged glances. "There is the threat of war."

"Uh huh." I'd heard that before.

"Humans are encroaching on our hereditary hunting territory."

"Right... They just managed to get their trawlers through the magic portal? That would certainly be newsworthy." Also: impossible.

The merfolk's home was protected by several layers of ancient enchantments same as any other magical society. To even get close someone had to be granted a boon and given an invitation by someone with magic in their blood, and even then a normal human wasn't likely to survive.

A screaming six-year-old went tearing past me, dove into the water with all the grace of a flailing crocodile, and rose above the surf holding a two-foot-long dogfish who was frantically trying to escape in the politest way possible.

"Put that down!" I ordered my son.

"Animals aren't that's." My son unceremoniously flipped the little shark over to look at its belly and claspers. "He's a boy."

"He has boy parts," I corrected. "Gender is a social construct."

No, I don't know why I said something so inane. Let's say it was panic. I came to the beach to relax, to take a day off of farm chores, to feel the delicious sea breeze. Not to watch my youngest child humanhandle a terrified guardian of the deep who was bent on ensuring my rise to empress of the world's oceans.

Parenting books do not cover situations like this.

"Put the fish down."

"Shark," my son corrected. "He's not technically a fish." But he put the magical creature back in the water anyway.

"Go back to your father and play in the sea grass," I said.

He sighed, kicked at a wave that was playfully jumping on him, and looked up at me. "Do you think there's any sunken treasure here?"

"What do you want? Pirate treasure? Doubloons? Pearls?"

His small face squinched up in thought. "How about a sailor's compass with barnacles?"

"Sure." Easy enough. "Go play in the sea grass and see if you can find it."

Ray scowled at me.

"What? I said I didn't want to rule, not that I wouldn't use my powers for my own amusement!"

"It's a tasteless abuse of power."

"So? I'm supposed to be the villain! The Dread Empress Of All The Oceans is my unofficially official title. I'm supposed to take the throne so you can overthrow me and keep your bargain to defend the watery kingdom of whatever the heck you call it."

He rolled his eyes.

Look, I have small children who go to a rural school in the Bible Belt. If I start cussing they start cussing and then I have to look at the principal and explain why my daughter knows how to say "F*ck Your Mother" in sixteen languages.

And I'm already in trouble for letting the oldest one do a class project on misogyny in history textbooks.

Or was it because I told her to use singular they?

Whichever it was, I like to go whole days without being called to the school so they can complain about my parenting choices. Although it is nice to see that the pastor's wife stopped wearing fur to the PTS meetings since our last protest.

Ray grumbled under his breath. "You are destined to shake the world."

"Yes, and I am. Up here. On land. Where I can shake it for a good reason and help people. Being pure evil isn't fun, really. That's why my many-times-great-grandmother made the trade and gave up her siren voice for legs."

It's also why my family regarded *The Little Mermaid* as a necessary evil but avoided watching it whenever possible. The fact that Ariel *was* the Wicked Sea Witch is way more interesting than anything Disney could come up with.

Cursing in a language that would turn normal humans into sobbing wrecks, Ray turned away. "How about a vacation then? One week of evil ruling and we end it by throwing you out of the castle?"

"With a spear in my chest?"

"It's traditional."

"No thanks. Find someone else. I hear there are some people in D.C. who would make great evil overlords for you to kill."

His smile brightened. "You think so?"

I nodded enthusiastically. "Oh. Yes. For sure." I waved as he left and went to see what my family had found in the sea grass.

The small green bucket we had brought with us had several empty co-quina shells, pink pearls, a small dagger suitable for a lady, and a compass covered in barnacles.

"Everything go well?" my husband asked as he welcomed me back with a hug and a kiss.

"Perfectly fine." I watched the tide settle and the sharks retreat. "In the spirit of open communication and honesty, I may have sorta kinda put a hit on some politicians in Washington."

My husband looked down at me with a worried expression.

"Maybe. I didn't name names or anything."

"Well that's… you know… eggs and omelets I suppose. Necessary sacrifices, etcetera etcetera." He kissed my head again. "It's not like they can trace it back to us."

"Exactly."

"And there are worse things you could do with your power."

"Precisely."

"It's not like you flooded the city just to get the shopping centers to yourself on Black Friday."

"Not this year."

"It's progress."

We watched our oldest spin in the water so it seemed to an imaginative eye that it almost formed a flowing dress around her.

Almost.

Probably not.

Best not to dwell on it, really.

"Maybe next year we should do something else for vacation," I said. "Go hiking. Hit the mountains."

"Sure, let's visit the Hall of the Mountain King. That worked so well for us last time."

"It was only a tiny battle," I said hopefully.

The Woodland King shook his head at me. "We left a national park burning."

"But the archers didn't steal the baby!" I tried to focus on the positives.

"How about New York?" he said. "There's lots of metal and plastic and nonmagical things. We could be very safe in a city like that."

I smiled and nodded weakly. "Yeah. Sure. No problems at all. It's not like there are Elder Gods or anything in New York." My laugh sounded forced but fortunately my husband was distracted by our twins trying to haul up a golden sword out of the sea grass.

For today, it didn't matter. We could play at the beach, have fun, spend time together as a family.

And when we got home we'd talk about my father's side of the family.

THE MAKING OF
DREAD EMPRESS OF ALL THE OCEANS

This is—more or less—a true story. The beach exists. So does the farm. I didn't have twins but I have the knee problems. The black and white swimsuit existed, although it has since retired. The only thing fictional is the merfolk and the inheritance.

While we lived in the panhandle of Florida, this little beach between the bay and the ocean was one of my family's favorite places to go swimming. It was safe for the little kids and had seagrass for the older kids to snorkel in. We never found any treasure, magic kingdoms, or sharks, but the barnacles are dangerous enough.

Read more by Liana Brooks!

ALL I WANT FOR CHRISTMAS IS A WEREWOLF

THERE WAS MISTLETOE OVER MY DESK. Honest to goodness mistletoe hanging over the remains of my Halloween festivities. The Great Pumpkin was now overshadowed by a hemiparasitic shrub.

When I'd left for a conference two hours ago, my desk had been a bastion against the winter holidays. A snow-free island in an otherwise elegantly decorated office suite dedicated to art.

The gallery's front foyer with the dark wood paneling and over-stuffed pine-green tub chairs was now dis-playing glass and metal snowflakes in dazzling designs.

The main negotiating room, with the long table suitable for a fleet of lawyers, had a festive Seasons Greetings banner with pine trees and bright red birds signed by various Miami athletes.

The hall had garlands, multi-colored lights, and occasionally holiday music blaring out of incautiously opened offices.

But this?

This monstrous greenery was not supposed to touch my space.

Elegant Miami's main art gallery across the MacArthur Causeway was a glittering gem of holiday art. But over here, at the offices on Miami Beach that had been selected specifically to be near my boss's favorite house, things were toned down.

This was where Elegant Miami hid the nitty gritty details of business. It was the safe space for the sales people that spent all day on the phone with overseas clients; it was the home base of the style teams who went and decorated Miami palaces with carefully curated art from around the world; it was a soulless sovereignty of the contracts office where Maureen and I made sure every jot and tittle were in place.

Tittle was one of my co-worker's favorite words. It means the dot over a lower case I or J, but it sounds funny. Stuck in an L-shaped, linoleum-floored concrete bunker with two high windows that looked at the neighboring building a foot away and that always smelled of nail polish and mildew, we took our fun where we could find it.

But I drew the line at plastic Naughty Santa window clings blocking the little sunlight available. Being held hostage by forced holiday cheer was not part of my paycheck.

"Happy holidays, Del!" Maureen jumped out from behind my desk wearing a bright blue sweater with silver bells, dancing elves, and snowflakes. The bell at the end of her bright pink

Santa hat with pole dancing elves jingled as she stilled.

I stared, carefully counting to ten in every language I could remember, willing the other half the contracts team to vanish. It wasn't enough. Maureen and her seasonal cheer remained where they were.

"Don't you love it? I'm going to spray some fake snow too!" She pointed around at the sad, red tinsel garlands hanging off the black filing cabinets and the tiny palm tree that was sagging under a strand of rainbow lights.

"That's really not necessary," I said carefully circling around the hazardous airspace of the parasitic plant of unwanted kisses.

What was Maureen even thinking? Who on earth was I going to kiss here? It was against my personal policy to kiss clients or married people. That left Rafael Kane, office grinch, as the only possible target of unwanted contact.

Granted, he was a hot and sexy Office Grinch, but he was also the person voted most likely to ruin a party. He didn't chitchat. He didn't get distracted. He didn't waste time talking to coworkers, going to long Friday lunches, or building friendships.

Rafael Kane went to work, smiled for his clients only, and made Elegant Miami over fifteen percent of our yearly profit. We all loved him for his sales acumen, and stunning good looks, but no one around here considered him a friend.

Very early on, I'd tried. But Rafael Kane had taken one look at me, snarled like I'd stabbed his grandma, and avoided me ever since.

Which suited me just fine.

I frowned. If Maureen thought there was any chance of an office romance, my desk would look like an ad for the Great Bridal Expo. I needed tiny white seed pearls and chiffon as much as I needed mistletoe, which was about as much as a shark needed a tuba.

My idea of a good date was streaming a good murder mystery. I liked crime shows, creepy horror movies, and all things Halloween. People joked that I was a pagan, but that wasn't exactly true. I just loved the idea of magic. It made sense to me.

I should have loved the idea of Santa, except I can't remember a time I wasn't poor, and Santa doesn't visit poor kids.

December was my own personal hell. No winter solstice bonfire would ever be big enough to burn away all my anger at the forced cheer, demand for gifts, and unseasonable expectations.

I wasn't making New Year's Resolutions, I did that on my birthday in July.

I wasn't meeting anyone under the mistletoe, I wasn't that desperate.

I wasn't going to participate in the annual gift exchange, because somehow I always wound up with the bar of soap stolen from the pay-by-the-hour motel down the street.

I would be skipping the party, hitting the white sand beaches of Miami with a pink drink in hand, and spending my three days off catching up on N.W. Gehson's *Serial Killerz* series.

Maureen moved out from behind my desk and pouted. All of five-foot-nothing, she was a cute, apple-shaped woman with sunset pink hair and perpetually purple lips from a permanent makeup choice she made thirty years ago when she was twenty-one, drunk, and planning to be an exotic dancer all her life.[1]

In the bright blue sweater, she

---

[1] She still dances under the name Cotton Candy every other Friday down at the Sugar Strip on 4th, if you're wondering.

looked like the world's glummest Sugar Plum Fairy. She was holding a shiny blue paper with the words "All I Want For The Holidays" and a blank space for a holiday wish on it.

If I ignored the paper, I might escape further holiday interrogations.

"I… I was just trying to be nice!" A huge tear shimmered in her eye.

"I know." I patted her shoulder and tried very hard not to look at the tattoo peeking above her collar that HR insisted she keep covered during work hours. "But I don't like Christmas."

"This year is going to be different!" Maureen assured, her smile turning on like a floodlight in turtle season. "I figured out why you don't like Christmas."

"Because it's a commercial farce to celebrate capitalism?"

"No, silly! Because you're single! No one's giving you the good gifts." She winked and tried to bump me with her hip, but since her head only comes up to my shoulder even in kitten heels, it didn't quite work.

I scooted around her and into my three-sided box of an office.

There were sparkly confetti snow-flakes covering the nameplate that had been a gift from one of my favorite metal-work artists.

Delinna Farmer was not a name that deserved to have snow on it. Especially fake snow.

Shaking the snow off the metal cut-out of my name, I smiled up at Maureen. "Really, Maureen, I'm fine."

"You will be!" She pulled a scroll of candy pink paper out of her cleavage so it unrolled in a long, curling list. "This is Auntie Maureen's list of acceptable bachelors in the greater Miami area."

"Maureen," I said, sitting down and giving her my very best glare, "if Rafael Kane is mentioned even once on that list, I will murder you. Right here and now. There will be blood all over your dancing elf sweater. No jury will convict me."

She rolled her eyes. "Tried that. Obviously there's chemistry there, but Rafe could have chemistry with a doorknob, so it doesn't matter." She put the list of names—written in pink and purple ink—on my desk. "Names. Numbers. Histories. Sizes."

"Siz—Oh!" I covered my mouth. "Sweet mother of pearl! Maureen! This is so invasive!" I crumpled the list up and dropped it in the recycling bin.

"A girl's got to know…"

"I do not need to know anyone's sizes!" I shouted as the door to the contracts office opened and the devil himself walked in.

Rafael's brown eyes went wide, his tan face frozen in a rictus of horror.

"I'm not participating in the company Christmas party and I'm not ordering the shirts," I said loudly, willing

Maureen to play along. Rafael might be the office grinch, but nobody gossiped as much as his people in the sales department. If he even guessed at the content of Maureen's list, I'd have every art gallery employee and intern in the greater Miami area sending me extra details.

Maureen, oblivious to the threat of Dick Pic Armageddon, crossed her arms over her ample chest. "Why not? What's wrong with the holiday party?"

"Because…" I scrambled for an excuse that wouldn't insult Maureen's party planning. "…I'm seeing some-one."

Rafael snorted in amusement as he shook his head and walked to our copy machine by the door. The sales department had a better one, one that could print posters and banners, but it was broken and the sales associates had been bouncing in and out of the contracts office all week. There was nothing like the holidays to convince the obscenely wealthy to drop hundreds of thousands of dollars on art.

"Oh, sweetie," Maureen said, grabbing my arm and leaning in for a sideways hug as she ignored Rafael. "You don't need to lie."

"I'm not," I lied. "I am in a relationship. And I think it's serious. We are talking about moving in together."

From the copier Rafael gave me a look of disbelief that said, *No one would ever live with you.*

Maureen patted my hand with a tiny sigh of pity. "Let me guess. His name is Nick 'The Closer' Claus and you ordered him from the toys department at Lady Things downtown? I've met him too." Her smile was wicked. "But he doesn't count as a dinner date."

Too. Much. Information.

Closing my eyes, I focused on the filing list I needed to finish today. Anything to get the image of my middle-aged co-worker gleefully bouncing through the adult toy store out of my head.

In my imagination, she wore a frilled pink skirt that barely covered her ample thighs. I shuddered.

My only option was to lie more, or to hope Rafael would step in to help me. "Maureen—"

"No!" Rafael shouted from across the room. "No more. Not until I leave. I do not need to hear this. Let me finish. Please. Five more pages!"

Just for that I wanted to play dirty, but encouraging Maureen would give me a heart attack. There was only one course of action left…

"I'm getting a dog," I said before the dick pics became porno subscriptions in my stocking. "I've been visiting the shelters and I'm planning to adopt one over the holidays."

Maureen's shoulders sagged. "Honey, that does not count."

"A dog will be more loyal than any man will!" I drew myself up, a furious dark queen with a mask of rage perfected after years of studying every campy Halloween vampire movie ever. Morticia Addams, eat your heart out. "Probably more loyal than a woman, too. It'll love me, wait for me, and cuddle with me while I watch horror movies in December. A dog won't make me watch cheesy Christmas specials. A dog will go for walks on the beach with me. A dog will be happy eating whatever I cook—"

"A dog should have a high-protein diet."

Maureen and I both turned to stare.

Had Rafael Kane actually joined a conversation that wasn't about sales? After all these years?

"Do you like dogs?" Maureen asked politely, reverting back to Sweet Office Eccentric like a chameleon. "You've never mentioned them."

Rafael stared at the wall behind the copier as he realized his mistake. His body went rigid and I swear I saw a shiver of terror shimmy through him. He knew Maureen would never let him escape now.

"My mother raised dogs when I was growing up." He finished his copy work and turned to glare at me. "I've seen the stuff you eat for lunch, Del. Do the world a favor and stick to stuffed animals and battery-operated toys. A dog deserves better." He opened his mouth as if he were going to continue, then snapped it shut and marched out, back stiff.

Maureen hummed happily. "He has such a nice tush!"

"Maureen!" I smacked her arm.

"What? I'm married, not dead."

"We're at work."

"Quitting time was eight minutes ago. I can lust after people off the clock."

"You are a dirty old woman."

"Yes I am," she said proudly.

I rolled my eyes and remembered why I'd come back in. "I need to get my water bottles. I keep forgetting them." Nine of them sat in a row by my spare shoes.

"Oh, is that what happened?" Maureen asked. "I thought you'd decided to decorate with them. Maybe make a shrine to your beloved *agua*."

"Ha ha, funny." I grabbed a big bag with the name of a local farmer's stall on it and stuffed the water bottles inside. "The winter wonderland stuff. Can you keep it off my desk?"

Maureen pouted again.

"Please? I'll bring you some of those spiced pecans you like." If the bodega had a BOGO sale going on. If it wasn't buy-one-get-one, I wasn't sharing.

Her eyes went wide with delight. "Consider it gone. I will leave your corner a natural wasteland of bones, ghouls, and whatever that thing is," she said pointing to my Zany Zombie bobblehead.

"Thank you." I packed up and went home to research animal shelters. If I was going to be forced to participate in the holidays, I deserved to have someone who was happy to see me every day.

Surely I could get a dog for Christmas. It couldn't be that hard.

Keep reading! Head to www.inkprintpress.com/liana brooks/christmas/werewolf/ to buy your copy now!

ABOUT THE AUTHOR

While LIANA BROOKS has never been offered a kingdom under the sea to rule, she makes up for that by deftly inventing her own. In particular, Liana enjoys writing science fiction in every form, from sprawling space operas romances (the *Fleet of Malik* series) to the antics of a super-powered family (the *Heroes and Villains* series).

Liana also maintains a soft spot for paranormal romances. She writes the popular *All I Want For Christmas* novellas, including *All I Want For Christmas Is A Werewolf* and *All I Want For Christmas Is A Reaper*.

You can learn more about her and her books at www.LianaBrooks.com.

INKLETS

Collect them all! Released on the 1st and 15th
of each month.

Shadows
NEVER LIE
AMY LAURENS

Here She Lies
LIANA BROOKS

Perfect
Destruction
An Age Of Unicorns Story
AMY LAURENS

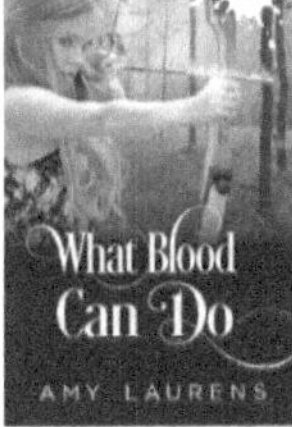

What Blood
Can Do
AMY LAURENS

Dancer, Dreamer
Seer
LIANA BROOKS

As Time
Whirls Slowly
Past
AMY LAURENS

Far More
Satisfying
Than Hell
AMY LAURENS

Just
Another Day
In Hell
LIANA BROOKS

Moon AND
Morning
AMY LAURENS

INKLET #088
Some Impropriety Expected
AMY LAURENS

INKLET #089
NEON SNOW
LIANA BROOKS

INKLET #090
Reincarnation
LIANA BROOKS

INKLET #091
More Than Mushrooms
AMY LAURENS

DOUBLE ISSUE
INKLET #092
How To Make A Star & The World Ended
LIANA BROOKS

INKLET #093
CAUGHT IN THE ACT
AMY LAURENS

INKLET #094
ANUBIS Has Sent You Six Souls
LIANA BROOKS

INKLET #095
PRAYER TO A GODDESS
LIANA BROOKS

INKLET #096
Love In The Time Of Corona
AMY LAURENS